Henry, the Owl who Says WHY?

JEFF TULLY
&
WRIGLEY ROSE TULLY

ILLUSTRATED BY OLGA ZHURAVLOVA
DESIGN BY HEATHER MCINTYRE

WELCOME!

After you finish
reading, see
the back
page to
answer all
those

WHYS?

And think of some
WHYS?
of your own

There are many
different types of owl.
Some hoot, some
screech, some even howl.

Owls live in trees and barns and even caves too.
No matter where they live though,
all owls say "WHO?"

All owls that is, except one small fry.
Henry is the only owl who says,

"WHY?"

Henry's very first "WHY" came without warning...
When Mama Owl woke her kids early one morning.

"My sweet children, I hope your dreams were nice.
Give me a 'WHO' if you'd like some fresh mice."

Henry hooted...

"Mama, WHY do we have to eat mice?
It's kind of gross and not very nice."

"Oh Henry, I never thought of that.
Would you prefer I serve you some rat?"

The mice cheered, "Yay! Rats are much better!
May we suggest that you try one with cheddar?"

Henry chirped, "Mom, please no rats in my belly.
WHY can't we just have some toast and grape jelly?"

Mama said, "Henry, you made me think twice.
From now on in this nest, we no longer eat mice."

"Hooray Henry, bless your sweet soul!"
Exclaimed all three mice inside the bowl.

After that, "WHY?" was Henry's favorite word to say.
And he said it one hundred times each & every day.

He asked serious questions like,
"WHY does rain sprinkle?"

And he asked silly questions like, "WHY do we tinkle?"

Finally, one day...
Mama had to say,
"Dear Henry, I don't have time for another WHY.
Please go find your Papa and learn how to fly."

So, Henry hopped to meet
his Papa for lessons.

Making stops on the way
to ask animals questions.

"WHY do you sleep all
winter, Mother Bear?"

"Because in winter,
there's no food to spare.
So, I sleep until spring
when the salmon are running."

Henry had more questions,
but he heard a loud humming.

"I hate to
bother you,
Miss Hummingbird...
But, WHY do you
make that sound I heard?"

"It's the sound my wings make
to hover over flowers.
When they're humming,
I can sip nectar for hours."

"Mister Porcupine, WHY are your quills
sharp and prickly?"

"Well, I couldn't scare off
wolves if they were
soft and tickly."

"Chippy Chipmunk,
WHY do both
of your cheeks
puff?"
"They have
stretchy membranes
to fit lots of stuff. And, that's why we
can carry more than one nut."
"Cool!
Mister Moth, WHY are there
lights on your butt?"
"I'm not a moth, kid. I'm called a Firefly.
...and bioluminescence is the reason WHY.
It helps us attract
our mate and
find true love."
"That's great.
And LOOK,
your light spotted
my Dad above!"

And sure enough, there was his Papa
high up in the trees.

His head was turned 'round –
one hundred and eighty degrees.

"Papa, WHY do you do that
with your head?

WHY don't you just turn
your body instead?"

Papa hooted,
"I turn my head 'round to catch predators lurking.
And I've spotted a fox, so it's time to start working.
Warning the forest is what we owls do.
Now it's your turn, Henry...Give me a WHO."

In his defense, Henry really did try.
But instead, out popped a very loud,

"WHY do badgers have that stripe on their fur?"

The Fox chimed in,
"I can answer that
young sir."

Papa Owl swooped his great wings down on the fox.
Nearly scaring that red villain out of his socks.

Papa screeched,
"Next time, you get the talons if you talk to my son!
And I assure you Fox, you won't find that much fun."

Fox barked back,
"He's safe, it's for the rest of your family I fear.
Look at your nest, a cast of hawks circles quite near."

"Henry, I must go to chase off those hawks.
While I'm gone don't say a word to that Fox."

"Yes Papa, I'm zipping my beak.
Starting now, I no longer speak."

Fox waited until Papa Owl flew far away.
Then, he stepped out and had this to say...

"Henry, please listen,
there's nothing to fear."

But, Henry turned his head
so he couldn't hear.

So Fox yipped...
"Do you know why moss grows on a tree's north side?"

Before he could stop, Henry's beak opened wide.

... blurted Henry, slapping a wing over his mouth.

"Because the sun would dry it out if it grew on the south."

Henry said, "That's very interesting Fox, I must admit."

Fox replied, "Ask me anything. You're safe where you sit."

After many questions – Henry reached his last, "WHY."

"Mr. Fox, WHY do all creatures describe you as sly?"

"Being sly means to play tricks, and that I can do. For this is the trick I've been playing on you.

While you were asking your questions of me.
My friend Badger was climbing right up your tree."

And there indeed, two eyes emerged from the trunk.
When he saw the Badger, Young Henry's heart sunk.

He looked down at the Fox from oh-so-up-high...
And the only word Henry said was of course,

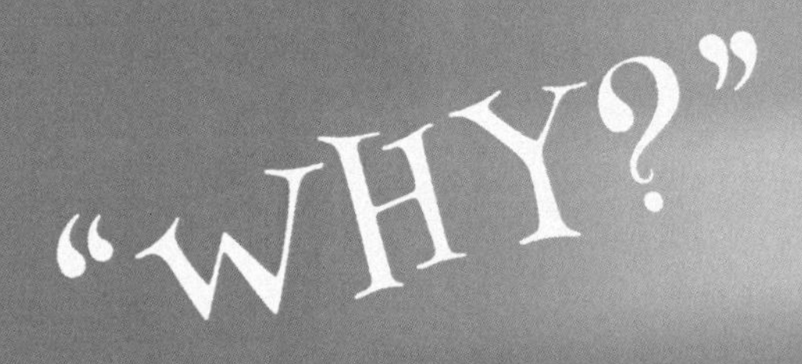

Fox said, "No more 'WHYS' and no more questions.
All I want from you now are serving suggestions."

Badger hissed as he closed in for his attack.
"This bird is small, but he'll make a nice snack."

Henry squawked...
"You'll have no SNACK,
I'm not sorry to say.
For lunch all you'll get
is a big SNAP today."

The Fox grinned wide – like the Cheshire Cat.
"To use your word Henry, just 'WHY' is that?"

Henry hooted,
"Hey Badger, do you hear that sound; like sawing?
On this branch, my mouse friends have been gnawing.
Thanks to them this limb is about to SNAP.

That's WHY it's you, Mr. Fox,
WHO fell into MY TRAP."

Sly Fox's smile then turned to a pout.

The mice stopped chewing.

SNAP!

Badger fell out.

He landed like a bag of rocks.
Right on top of the naughty Fox.

Henry shouted,
"Sorry to drop you out of the tree.
But, it really was you two rascals
– or me."

Fox crawled from under Badger,
his hungry lips parted...
"You're free to go Henry,
I've clearly been outsmarted.
Please, don't be angry with me for trying.
If it wasn't for me,
you wouldn't be flying."

Henry looked down
and the fox didn't lie.
For the very first time,
the young owl could

FLY.

As Henry soared home,
Fox heard him say...

"WHY aren't you angry that I got away?"

"Because..." Fox replied, "No matter how yummy,
I'd get sick of you asking
'WHY?'
from my tummy.

And most important, the world needs more WHYS.
This forest is a better place with you in her skies."

"Goodbye Fox," called Henry, as he flew over the moon.

"Goodbye Henry. I hope that we can chat again soon."

After giving it some careful thought.
Henry said, "Sure Mister Fox...

"WHY NOT?"

Why was Papa Owl angry?

Why is Fox waving?

Why do the mice love Henry?

Why do chipmunks have puffy cheeks?

Why do porcupines have quills?

Why do most owls say "Who?"

Why do you love your mom?

Why do hummingbirds hum?

Why do fireflies have lights?

Why were the mice chewing?

Why is your dad awesome?

Why do bears hibernate?

Why did you like this book?

JEFF TULLY

Jeff Tully is a television writer/producer. His first TV show was "The Daily Habit" on FUEL TV, an extreme sports comedy show your "older skateboarder cousin" probably watched.

WRIGLEY ROSE TULLY

Wrigley Rose Tully is currently a 6 year-old girl who was the inspiration for Henry. She not only also says, "Why?" an awful lot, but she also LOVES animals. In 2016, Wrigley received a special "Animal Protector" award from "Actors & Others for Animals" for helping rescue an injured hawk.

"Actors and Others for Animals" is a California non-profit corporation dedicated to the promotion of the humane treatment of animals. A portion of the proceeds of this book will go to that foundation in the names of our pals, Fred & Mary Willard. http://www.actorsandothers.com

Printed in the United States of America
First Printing, 2017
Copyright Case # 1-5736218671

ISBN-13: 978-19741685583
ISBN-10: 1974168581

Tullyvision Productions

https://jefftullyvision.wixsite.com/henrysayswhy

Illustrations: Olga Zhuravlova
Design and Typesetting: Heather McIntyre, Cover&Layout, www.coverandlyout.com

Made in the USA
San Bernardino, CA
20 September 2017